CALLIE ASKS FOR HELP

Based on the episode written by Mike Kramer

Adapted by Annie Auerbach

Illustrated by Premise Entertainment

DISNEY PRESS

Los Angeles • New York

Copyright © 2015 Disney Enterprises, Inc. All rights reserved. Published by Disney Press, an imprint of Disney Book Group. No part of this book may be reproduced or transmitted in any form or by any means, electronic or mechanical, including photocopying, recording, or by any information storage and retrieval system, without written permission from the publisher. For information address Disney Press, 1101 Flower Street, Glendale, California 91201.

First Paperback Edition, August 2015 10 9 8 7 6 5 4 3 2 1
ISBN 978-1-4847-1631-1

G658-7729-4-15170

Library of Congress Control Number: 2015933057

Manufactured in the USA
For more Disney Press fun, visit www.disneybooks.com

SUSTAINABLE
FORESTRY
INITIATIVE

Certified Chain of Custody
Promoting Sustainable Forestry

www.sfiprogram.org
SFI-01415
The SFI label applies to the text stock

Sheriff Callie likes to help.
Sparky likes to help, too.

"Help!" yells Farmer Stinky.
It's Callie and Sparky to the rescue.

Callie helps Farmer Stinky.
They paint the barn.

More friends need help.

Go, Callie! Go, Sparky!

Callie and Sparky help Dirty Dan.
They move a big rock.

Callie helps Priscilla.
She finds Priscilla's hat.

Ella asks for help.
There is a fight at her saloon.
Bo asks for help.
His jackalopes ran away!

Go, Callie! Go, Sparky!

Which milk shake is best?
Strawberry or banana?
No one can agree.
Callie mixes them together. Yum!

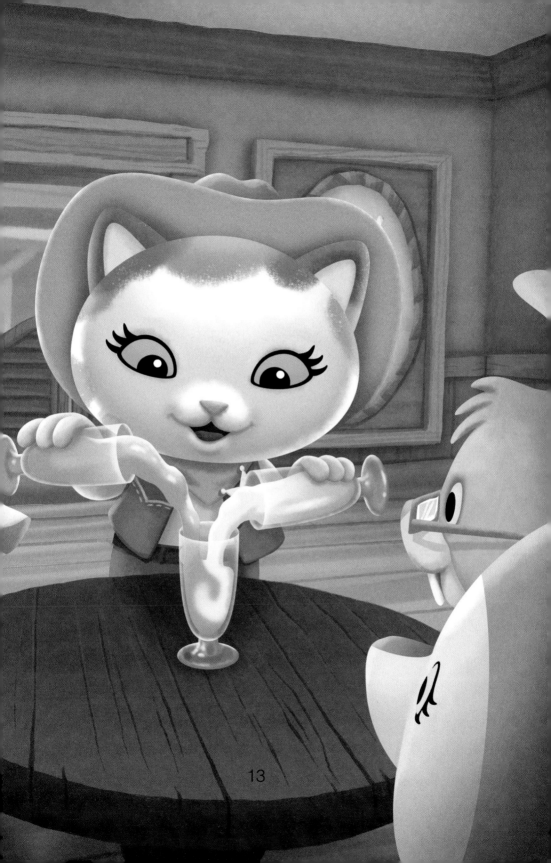

13

The jackalopes are getting away!

Callie brings them back.

Callie and Sparky run back and forth.
Sparky's feet dig a hole.
The hole becomes a canyon.
Soon Callie and Sparky are stuck!

Callie throws her lasso.
It does not work.

18

They jump up high.
But it is not high enough.

They are still stuck.
Callie and Sparky need help!

Callie writes a note on her hat.
She asks for help.

Please HELP!
We are stuck in a
deep canyon!
Sheriff Callie
and Sparky

They send the hat into the air.

Go, hat!

Please HELP!
We are stuck in a
deep canyon!
Sheriff Callie
and Sparky

The hat lands on Peck!

Peck calls his friends.

"Callie and Sparky need help!" he says.

They find Callie and Sparky.
How can they help?

Callie throws the lasso.
Everyone helps pull.

Callie and Sparky are safe!

"Thank you," says Callie.

She is happy she asked for help.

This place has a new name.
It is called Helping Hand Canyon!